There are piggies
in the woods…

The campsite was a mess. It had been trashed by the previous campers and looked nothing like what Virginia had imagined. She had expected a lush green meadow with a babbling brook running through the middle.

Instead, the campsite was a wreck! Mr. Hamhock and the girls got out of the minivan to survey the damage. There were empty cans and garbage strewn across the ground. The fire pit rocks had been moved, and there were half burnt logs lying everywhere. Bread bags, empty pudding cups and used plastic forks littered the trees. It looked as though a tornado had ripped through the campsite just before the scouts arrived.

PIGGY NATION
LET'S GO
CAMPING

RICHARD ROSSER
ILLUSTRATED BY SHANE SOWELL

For information regarding permission, contact
Piggy Nation Press
15332 Antioch Street Suite 419
Pacific Palisades, CA 90272
email richard@piggynation.com
or call 1-888-55PIGGY (557-4449)

Publisher's Cataloging-in-Publication Data
Rosser, Richard
Piggy nation: let's go camping / Richard Rosser;
illustrated by Shane Sowell
p. cm.

Summary: Virginia's dad volunteers to lead her scout troop on a
campout. The scouts learn about piggy behavior.
ISBN 978-0-983-99310-0
[1. Manners - Fiction. 2. Pigs - Fiction. 3. Scouts - Fiction.
4. Camping - Fiction.] I. Sowell, Shane, ill. II. Title.
2011916914

First Edition-2011
Printed in China

For Rex
Who loved the outdoors

Thanks to
Ali, Stacey, Linda and May
Jennifer and Alyssa
Maureen and Larry
Dave (D.W.)
Girl Scout Troops 6125 and 3965
Phil and Vera
Hank and Ann
Susan and Wendell
Harriet and Steve
Renee and Michael
Anne, Pepper, Caroly and Susan
Audrey, Dee and Bradley
Lise, Susan and Teresa
Collin and Austin
Araceli, Hector, Chris and Samantha
DJ, John, Craig, Read, Terry, Patrick, Ben and Bill
Dan, Jill, Geoff and Andrus
Tricia, Lauren and Reasha
Wes, Julie and Alex

CONTENTS

The Last Troop Meeting

Virginia Hamhock entered the auditorium and chucked her book bag in the corner. The bell had barely finished ringing, but school was already the farthest thing from her mind.

It was time for her scout troop meeting, the last one of the school year. Soon, Virginia and her friends would graduate from fifth grade. Next year they would be sixth graders, newbies at the middle school, and Cadette Scouts.

Virginia and her best friend, Rebecca Raccoonsby, joined scouts when they were in kindergarten. Olivia Longneck and Brianna Beaverton joined when they were in first grade.

Francesca Foxworthy and Lacey Leppàrd joined in second grade.

The scouts took their seats in the school gym. Mrs. Oxley, their den leader, called out, "Quiet down girls, we have a lot to cover today."

Rebecca looked at Virginia and made a funny face. Virginia stifled a laugh and stared at Mrs. Oxley, trying to hold a straight face.

"This weekend is the fifth grade overnight," said Mrs. Oxley, smiling. "I know you're all excited."

The fifth grade overnight was the end of the scout experience in elementary school. The girls had looked forward to the campout since kindergarten!

Mrs. Oxley handed a stack of forms to Lacey, who was seated in the front row, "These are medical release forms. Have a parent sign one, and return it tomorrow. No form, no trip."

Olivia leaned over and whispered to Virginia and Rebecca, "My brother told me that a girl got left behind on last year's campout."

Rebecca looked shocked, "Really?"

Olivia nodded, "She was stuck in the woods for three days."

"No way," objected Virginia.

"Yes, way," responded Olivia. "My brother said they had to airlift her out with a helicopter."

Virginia and Rebecca shared a tentative glance, not sure whether to believe Olivia.

"Was she okay?" Rebecca asked.

Olivia nodded, "Yes, but she nearly starved to death."

Virginia countered, "I think your brother made the whole thing up. Like when he told us that 'Bubble Yum' bubble gum has spider eggs in it."

Olivia smirked, "He did *not* make it up."

"Did too," argued Virginia.

"Did not."

"Did too."

Mrs. Oxley raised her voice, "Pay attention, girls. What I have to say next is very important."

As Virginia and Rebecca turned their attention back to Mrs. Oxley, Olivia whispered, "Did not."

Olivia always had to get in the last word. It was something that annoyed Virginia, but she was fun otherwise.

Mrs. Oxley continued, "This camping trip is the last chance you'll have to earn badges. As you know, you must earn thirty badges in order to make Cadette Scout." She looked at her clipboard and announced, "Francesca, you currently have twenty-eight badges. Congratulations! You only need to earn two badges on the camping trip."

3

Francesca Foxworthy, kids called her Franny, was a tomboy and loved all things sports and outdoors. Virginia and Franny had played soccer together since first grade. Their team, the Powder Puffs, won the league championship in fourth grade when Franny scored two goals against the Atomic Fireballs. Virginia guessed that most of Franny's badges were for sports or other outdoor activities.

Mrs. Oxley continued down the list, "Brianna, you have twenty-seven badges. Very nice."

Brianna spent most of her time in the library reading or studying. She was shy. The only time Virginia had spoken to Brianna was when she needed help on a math problem.

Next on the list was Rebecca, with twenty-six badges. She and Virginia were best friends. They had known each other since preschool, and spent so much time together that sometimes they finished each other's sentences.

Olivia and Lacey both had twenty-five badges. They would each have to earn five badges on the camping trip. Mrs. Oxley commented, "You girls have your work cut out for you, but I have faith that you'll earn enough badges."

Mrs. Oxley's finger settled at the bottom of the list. She frowned. Virginia slid down in her chair.

She knew who was last. Mrs. Oxley looked up from her clipboard and called out, "Miss Hamhock."

"Yes," replied Virginia meekly.

"You have only earned twenty-two badges."

Virginia slunk lower in her seat. It had been a difficult year. The flu had cost her the Hobby and Jeweler badges. A family reunion had cost her the Water Fun badge because she hadn't been able to attend a scout trip to the beach.

Finally, she spent a weekend studying for a math test and missed a farm trip where the other girls earned their Farming and Horse Rider badges.

If Virginia hadn't missed all of those events, she and Brianna would be tied with twenty-seven badges. There was a chance that Virginia might not earn enough badges to make Cadette Scout.

Virginia thought the beach field trip would have been more fun than the family reunion, which consisted of distant aunts and uncles pigging out on coleslaw and potato salad. She wished there was a badge for attending boring events.

Mrs. Oxley tapped her pen on the clipboard and stated the obvious, "You're in danger of not making Cadette Scout."

Virginia sighed. Mrs. Oxley continued, "You have to earn eight badges on the camping trip this weekend, nearly an impossible task. You know, the record is eight badges, set by my daughter Margaret."

All of the girls knew about Margaret Oxley. Although Margaret was ten years older than Virginia, she served as the benchmark for achievement. She had been the perfect scout, the perfect dancer, the perfect athlete and the perfect student.

The girls had heard about Margaret Oxley since they started elementary school. Margaret was a favorite subject of all the teachers and parents, especially her own mother, Mrs. Oxley. Virginia and her friends were tired of hearing about Margaret.

"You'll have to tie my daughter's record in order to make Cadette Scout," said Mrs. Oxley. "Good luck. It'll be quite a challenge."

Mrs. Oxley handed another stack of papers to Lacey.

"This is a checklist of the items you'll need for the campout," said Mrs. Oxley. "You can bring a sleeping bag and a small duffel bag. That's it. If something doesn't fit in the duffel, you'll leave it behind."

"Also, no electronics of any kind are allowed on the campout." Olivia was half paying attention as she texted on her phone. Mrs. Oxley glared at her and continued, "That means no cell phones Miss Longneck. No video games, music players or laptops."

The girls groaned. It was one thing to be in the woods all weekend, but no music or communication would be brutal. Virginia considered this and realized there probably wouldn't be a cell signal anyway. Oh well, if she were going to earn eight badges, she wouldn't have time for texting.

Virginia looked at the list and wondered how she'd fit all the items into a single duffel bag. She took a copy and handed the stack to Rebecca.

"Unfortunately, I'll be unable to supervise the camping trip," said Mrs. Oxley. "My daughter, Margaret, graduates from college this weekend. She's Phi Beta Kappa, Summa Cum Laude and Valedictorian." Virginia didn't know what all of that mumbo jumbo meant, but she was certain Margaret was still setting records even though she was in college.

"I checked the parent volunteer schedule," Mrs. Oxley continued. "Mrs. Hamhock and Mrs. Leppàrd signed up to supervise the campout this weekend."

The girls cheered. Virginia's mom worked as an event planner. Whenever she volunteered, the outing turned into a party.

The previous year, Mrs. Hamhock organized a book club event, complete with a chocolate fountain. Two years prior, the beach cleanup included a moon bounce and a slip and slide!

There was no telling what Mrs. Hamhock would do for the camping trip. The scouts might feast on shrimp cocktails, or maybe Virginia's mom would decorate the campsite with streamers and balloons. Whatever it was, the girls were guaranteed a weekend of fun!

An Alternate Plan

"I can't supervise a camping trip this weekend," yelled Mrs. Hamhock. Her head was inside the fridge as she put away a half-gallon of milk. "The Nichols wedding is Saturday and the Abrams' baby shower is Sunday afternoon."

"But Mom," pleaded Virginia. "You signed up to volunteer at the beginning of the school year. You can't back out now!"

Mrs. Hamhock's head popped out of the fridge. "Sorry, honey. I've been planning the Nichols wedding for six months. One of the other scout mothers will have to volunteer. I'll call Mrs. Oxley. Why don't you finish putting these groceries away?"

As Virginia put a cereal box in the cupboard, her mom called Mrs. Oxley. "Hi Myrna, this is Ida Mae Hamhock." Virginia grabbed a carton of eggs from the grocery bag as her mom spoke, "I have some bad news. The camping trip never made it on my calendar. I have to work all weekend."

Virginia placed the eggs quietly into the fridge, listening carefully as her mom continued, "Can you ask one of the other mothers?" Virginia could hear the muffled sound of Mrs. Oxley's voice from the phone. "What about Freda Foxworthy?" asked Virginia's mother. There was a pause as Mrs. Oxley spoke. Virginia hoped the answer would be yes, but the expression on her mom's face said no.

"Could you ask Bonnie Beaverton, or Rachel Raccoonsby?" asked Mrs. Hamhock. Her silence told Virginia that there was no solution. Mrs. Hamhock listened intently and replied, "I see. Well, I hope it doesn't come to that."

Virginia stared at her mom and mouthed, "Come to what?" Her mom put her finger up as if to say, "Hold on." She continued listening to Mrs. Oxley.

Virginia's dad entered the kitchen, dressed in his uniform. Mr. Hamhock worked as a Piggy Patrol Officer. It was his job to snout out piggy behavior. Things like letting a pet poop on a neighbor's lawn,

11

parking in two spaces or talking too loudly on a cell phone. When Mr. Hamhock spotted piggy behavior, he gave the offender a Piggy Ticket.

Mr. Hamhock reached for an apple and patted Virginia on the head, "Hey, honeybunch. How was school?"

Virginia shushed her dad and pointed to her mom on the phone.

He whispered, "Sorry, what's going on?"

Virginia shushed her dad a second time as she struggled to hear Mrs. Oxley's response.

Mrs. Hamhock shook her head and replied, "That would be a shame. We'll keep our fingers crossed." She hung up the phone.

"What did she say?" sputtered Virginia.

"They might have to cancel the trip."

"No, way. They can't!"

Virginia couldn't believe this was happening. Her mom was the most organized person in the world. It's what she did for a living. She organized other people's lives. How could she have forgotten to put the camping trip on the family calendar?

Virginia erupted like a volcano, "This is all your fault. You and your stupid wedding. Now, I won't earn thirty badges and I'll never be a Cadette Scout. I'll be the laughing stock of middle school!"

12

She stormed out of the kitchen.

"What was that all about?" asked Mr. Hamhock.

Mrs. Hamhock explained, "I forgot to mark Virginia's scout campout on the calendar. I volunteered to supervise, but the Nichols wedding is this weekend. Mrs. Oxley may cancel the trip."

"Why don't you have one of the other mothers cover for you?"

"I tried, but everyone else is busy."

"Hmmm. Looks like you're in a bit of a jam," chuckled Mr. Hamhock as he popped the whole apple in his mouth.

Mrs. Hamhock shook her head, "I just need someone who's free this weekend to take my place and supervise the campout."

A grin spread across Mr. Hamhock's face.

His wife noticed and asked, "What are you grinning for?"

"I'm available."

"You?" Mrs. Hamhock asked. "What do you know about camping?"

Mr. Hamhock scoffed, "My grandfather took me camping every weekend when I was a piglet."

"You haven't been camping for over twenty years."

Mr. Hamhock remembered camping with his grandfather: the sound of rocks crunching under boots on the hiking trail; the smell of burning wood from a roaring campfire; fishing in the lake at twilight; the taste of freshly cooked trout and baked beans; sleeping under the stars.

However, Mr. Hamhock forgot to remember: blisters on his hooves after hiking miles to the campsite; mosquitoes as big as jet planes; smoke stinging his eyes until he wailed like a baby; being scared so badly by howling coyotes that he cried himself to sleep.

"So," Mr. Hamhock countered. "Have you ever been camping?" There was a silent pause. He knew the answer was no. "You volunteered to supervise a weekend campout, but you've never been camping. How hard could it be?"

"This is a scout troop. Of girls," she replied.

"I chaperoned the class trip to the state fair. There were girls on that trip," he argued.

"But this would be for the whole weekend."

"You think I can't handle a couple of girls?" he snorted.

"Girls are different from boys," replied Mrs. Hamhock. "They can be very… difficult."

Mr. Hamhock smiled, "Call Mrs. Oxley and tell

her you found a replacement."

Mrs. Hamhock hesitated. Although she wanted desperately to please Virginia, she had reservations about letting her husband supervise a troop of girls in the woods for two days. He had a habit of messing things up.

She remembered the time he took Virginia to sell scout cookies. As Virginia was selling a box of cookies to their elderly neighbor, Mrs. Turtleton, Mr. Hamhock backed over her mailbox while giving a neighbor a Piggy Ticket.

Then, there was the time he chaperoned their son's field trip to the natural history museum. Mrs. Hamhock never got the complete story, but somehow her husband knocked over the Tyrannosaurus Rex skeleton.

It took a team of paleontologists three months to reconstruct the T-Rex exhibit. As a result, their son's school had been banned from future field trips to the museum.

As Mrs. Hamhock weighed the pros and cons of the situation, she realized there was one consolation, every scout outing required two grownup volunteers. That meant there would be another mother going on the camping trip to help supervise the girls and Mr. Hamhock.

"Okay, I'll call Mrs. Oxley," said Mrs. Hamhock.

Mrs. Oxley wasn't crazy about the idea, but relented when she realized they were out of options.

"Alright," said Mrs. Hamhock as she hung up the phone. "Mrs. Oxley said you can take my place."

Mr. Hamhock whooped, "Alright!"

"On one condition," his wife continued. "You have to remember that you're supervising a troop of girls. Be patient with them. This campout is supposed to be a learning experience. I want you to leave your Piggy Patrol uniform at home and make it a fun trip."

Mr. Hamhock nodded, "No problem. We're gonna have a blast!" He rushed out of the kitchen, yelling, "Virginia, pack your stuff! We're going camping!"

Packing for the Trip

Virginia was so excited, it only took her fifteen minutes to pack for the camping trip. Despite her initial concerns, everything on the checklist fit neatly in her duffel bag. She rolled her sleeping bag and set it on top of the duffel, ready for the weekend.

Unfortunately, her dad wasn't so productive. Virginia found him in the attic, scrounging through old boxes of junk.

"I know my camping gear is here somewhere," he said, tossing aside an old fireplace tool. "I remember packing everything in a box and carrying it up here when we moved in."

He ripped open another box. It was full of

Tupperware containers, yellow with age. He held one up and muttered, "Look at this. It's worthless. Who would want to eat out of this thing?" He chucked the Tupperware back in the box and shoved the whole thing toward the door. "That Tupperware is headed for the garbage. In fact, I'll bet most of the stuff up here should be thrown away."

Virginia sensed a project coming on. Her dad was big on projects: cleaning the garage; re-organizing the broom closet; clearing out the cabinet under the bathroom sink…

A normal dad project usually took several hours, but the attic was endless. If they got sucked into the vortex of cleaning the attic, they would be up there for days. In fact, they might miss the campout altogether. Virginia had to act fast.

"I'm sure the box is here somewhere, let's keep looking," she said, ripping open another box filled with old car parts.

"You're right," replied her dad. He tossed aside a box of action figures.

A half hour later, Virginia and her dad struck gold. Buried underneath a pile of old piglet clothes was a large box marked *Camping Gear*.

"Eureka," exclaimed Virginia's dad. He ripped the box open like an excited kid on Christmas morning. He pulled a pocketknife out of the box and showed it to Virginia. "My grandfather gave me this pocketknife when I turned ten."

He handed the knife to Virginia. She examined it closely. The initials H.H. were engraved on the handle.

Mr. Hamhock smiled, "My grandfather engraved my initials on the handle before he gave it to me for my birthday," he said. "I used that knife to carve all sorts of stuff."

Virginia's dad reached into the box and pulled out a wooden bear, "I carved this bear at summer camp. It took me a whole month." He rubbed it with his thumb, remembering.

Out of the box came a compass, a pair of binoculars and a collapsible fishing rod. Virginia looked on in wonder. The box of camping gear was like a treasure chest.

Virginia's dad pulled out a camping pot. It was rusted and blackened with soot. He pried open the top to reveal several smaller pots nestled inside.

"Eeeeeew. Those are disgusting," squealed Virginia. The pots were covered with soot, rust and dried food. Her dad had packed the pots away without cleaning them. They'd been sitting in the box for nearly twenty years.

"They just need a good scrubbing and they'll be good as new," replied her dad. Virginia looked at the pots, doubtful that anything would get them clean enough to eat out of. She didn't want to hurt her dad's feelings, but those pots were definitely headed for the garbage.

He reached deep into the box and grinned, "Here's my old sleeping bag. Now we're in business." He pulled the sleeping bag from the box and shook it out. Feathers flew around the attic. Virginia and her dad coughed from the dust and feathers.

On closer inspection, Virginia saw that her father's sleeping bag was full of holes. Sometime during the twenty years of storage, a family of moths had dined on the sleeping bag, leaving it tattered and frayed.

Her dad laid the sleeping bag on the floor of the attic and surveyed the damage. Knowing her father, Virginia expected him to claim that the sleeping bag could be patched. To her surprise, he shook his head and said, "Looks like this sleeping bag has seen better days. It's headed for the trash."

Virginia offered, "Maybe you can borrow one from Rebecca's dad."

Her dad cringed, "I'm not using someone else's sleeping bag. What if he peed in it? Yuck."

He shoved the ragged sleeping bag back in the box and said, "We need to make a trip to the army supply store. I'll pick you up tomorrow after school and we'll go shopping for a new sleeping bag."

The army supply store was crammed with stuff from floor to ceiling. There were military uniforms, parachutes, snowshoes, flags and camping gear of all shapes and sizes. Virginia's dad was like a kid in a candy store. After wandering the aisles for an hour, he found the sleeping bags and decided on a model designed for a polar patrol with a temperature rating that would keep him warm to twenty degrees below zero.

As they headed to the register, Virginia's dad passed the camping aisle. He saw a new set of nesting pots. "My old pots are too far gone. Maybe we should get a new set," he said, loading the pots into his cart.

Several aisles later, the cart was loaded with a box of waterproof matches, several water bottles, a snakebite kit, first aid kit, insect repellant and sunscreen.

Virginia commented, "You know Dad, we're only allowed to bring a sleeping bag and one duffel bag on the campout."

"That rule is only for the girls in your troop," he responded. "I'm the leader. There's no limit to what I can bring." He proceeded to load the cart with a case of candles, a five-gallon water container, a hatchet, a hammock and a folding shovel.

As they approached the back of the store for the third time, Virginia asked, "Don't you think we have enough stuff, Dad? We're only going camping for the weekend."

Her father scoffed, "Do you know the Boy Scout motto?"

Virginia shook her head.

"The Boy Scout motto is *Be Prepared*," her dad continued. "But, that's not good enough for me. What if we're prepared, and something happens that we hadn't thought of? Then we're up a creek without a paddle. It's not good enough to be prepared. My motto is… *Be Over-Prepared*. Then, no matter what happens, we're prepared."

After her dad's speech, Virginia kept quiet. He loaded the cart with a portable shower, a water filtration kit, emergency space blankets, a case of bio-degradable toilet paper, a folding camp cot with mosquito netting, a flare gun, signal mirror, an assortment of bungee cords, a rope ladder and a can opener.

By the time Virginia and her dad reached the checkout counter, the cart was overflowing with gear. The bill came to $847.89.

The clerk asked, "Would you like to pay with cash or credit?"

Virginia's dad opened his wallet. Inside was a twenty-dollar bill, not enough to pay for the gear. He handed the clerk a credit card and said, "I'll pay with credit."

As the clerk processed the credit card, Mr. Hamhock shot Virginia a glance as if to say, "Please, don't tell your mom about this."

They're Late!

Finally, Saturday morning arrived. The scouts were to meet in the school parking lot at six. They wanted to get an early start on the two-hour drive to the campground.

Rebecca and her dad arrived at five forty-five and were waiting by the curb with her duffel and sleeping bag.

Brianna sat in her father's car reading. Her gear was neatly packed away in the trunk.

Mrs. Longneck had stopped to get coffee. Olivia sipped a large blended drink that would keep her active for hours.

Lacey and Franny arrived at five after. Another

ten minutes passed. Still, there was no sign of Virginia and her dad. Parents and daughters waited by their cars.

Rebecca's dad looked at his watch and asked Mrs. Longneck, "Where in the heck are they? The girls were supposed to leave at six."

Mrs. Longneck shrugged and sipped her coffee, "You got me."

Mr. Raccoonsby turned to Rebecca, "Why don't you text Virginia?"

"I can't text her. I don't have my phone."

"What?"

"Mrs. Oxley said no electronics."

Mr. Raccoonsby pulled out his cell phone, "I'll call her on my phone. What's her number?"

Rebecca shrugged, "I don't know. It's on speed dial in my phone."

Mr. Raccoonsby shook his head, "This is ridiculous." He turned to the girls. "Do any of you know Virginia's phone number?"

The girls shook their heads. Mr. Beaverton pulled his cell phone out of the holder on his belt and said, "I'll call information."

As he dialed, there was a loud clattering noise from down the street. Everyone turned to see the Hamhock minivan pulling a trailer piled with gear.

As the minivan pulled into the parking lot, the trailer scraped the asphalt with a loud screech that caused everyone to cover their ears.

The minivan pulled to a stop next to the other cars. Mr. Hamhock hopped out and approached the other parents, "I had trouble with my trailer hitch this morning, but I solved the problem."

Virginia got out of the minivan and joined her friends, who stared at the trailer.

"What is all that?" asked Rebecca.

Virginia sighed, "My dad went a little crazy at the army supply store."

"A little?" blurted Olivia. "He must've bought everything in the place!"

Virginia continued, "I convinced him that we wouldn't need gas masks or a parachute, but he bought everything else. He borrowed the trailer from our neighbor. I don't know if there's enough room for our stuff."

"Let's load the girls' gear and get on the road," said Virginia's dad as he grabbed several duffle bags and threw them on the trailer. Mr. Raccoonsby grabbed Rebecca's duffel and followed Mr. Hamhock's lead.

After securing the duffel bags with a bungee cord, Virginia's dad scanned the parking lot and asked, "Where's Mrs. Leppàrd?"

"She called at five this morning to ask if I could give Lacey a ride," said Mrs. Foxworthy. "Her son has a fever of a hundred and three."

Mr. Hamhock replied, "But, she volunteered to supervise the campout with me. There are supposed to be two adults." He looked at the other parents and asked, "Can one of you come along?"

"I'd go with you, but I have to coach my son's baseball game this afternoon," commented Mr. Raccoonsby.

Mrs. Foxworthy offered, "My younger daughter has a piano recital tomorrow morning. She'd be devastated if I missed it."

"I'm installing a deck in our backyard," said Mr. Beaverton. "I've been planning it for weeks."

Mrs. Longneck looked around and realized that all eyes were on her. She stammered, "My husband and I are going to dinner at that new restaurant, Shimmer. We made reservations three months ago."

"Looks like it's just you and the girls," Mr. Raccoonsby said as he opened his car door.

Mr. Beaverton looked over at the girls. He lowered his voice so the girls wouldn't hear him. He told Mr. Hamhock, "Everyone would understand if you decided to back out."

The other parents nodded in agreement.

Mr. Hamhock responded, "You're right. It would probably be smart to postpone the trip until we have two adults to supervise."

Virginia looked over from the group of girls and yelled, "Dad, what are we waiting for?"

Her dad called out, "Just a minute honey. We're going over some details."

Mr. Hamhock turned back to the parents and said, "The girls will be disappointed if we postpone the trip. I'll be fine by myself. We'll have a good time." He turned to the girls and yelled, "Who's ready for a campout?"

Six smiling faces responded, "We are!"

"To the van!" called Virginia's dad.

The girls rushed toward the minivan. Virginia yelled, "I call shotgun."

After a quick seatbelt check, Mr. Hamhock started the minivan, waved goodbye to the other parents and pulled out of the parking lot. The trailer scraped the asphalt a second time and the scouts were on their way.

As they drove toward the campsite, the girls discussed which badges they planned to earn. None of them had ever been camping before, so they were anxious at the prospect of being eaten by wild animals and ending up covered with poison oak hives.

Virginia's dad assured the girls that any wild animals they saw would be scared and run away. He told them that they would be safe as long as they stayed in a group.

He explained how to recognize poison oak so they could stay away from the plant. Just in case, there was calamine lotion in the first aid kit.

After an hour on the road, boredom set in. The girls wondered when they would arrive at the campsite. There was still an hour to go, the radio was out of range and there was no alternate form of entertainment since electronics had been banned from the trip.

Mr. Hamhock tried his best to think of an activity that might keep the girls entertained. He suggested, "You girls want to sing a song?"

"Nah," they responded.

"How about the billboard alphabet game?"

"Nah," they responded a second time.

He wondered if he had made a mistake taking the girls camping without another grown up. The trip might be harder than he thought. A car passed on the left. Mr. Hamhock noticed that the driver was eating a hamburger with both hands and steering with his knees.

"Look at that piggy behavior," blurted Mr. Hamhock. "That man is eating with both hands while driving on the freeway."

The girls moved to the left side of the van to get a better look.

"If I didn't have you girls along, I'd pull that guy over and write him a Piggy Ticket," said Virginia's dad. "The road is full of piggies. You just have to keep your eyes open."

The girls were suddenly energized. Their boredom disappeared. They examined passing vehicles for piggy behavior. Several minutes later, Olivia spotted a piggy driving a sedan.

"Look at that man. He's reading a book while driving."

"You're right, Olivia," responded Mr. Hamhock. "That's a violation of piggy civility code sixty-eight."

Sure enough, the man was driving while reading a book. Mr. Hamhock paced the car. The girls watched as the driver turned a page and continued reading… While driving on the freeway.

Several miles down the road, Lacey spotted a piggy driving an SUV.

"Look at that woman. She's putting on mascara while driving."

"Good spot, Lacey," said Virginia's dad.

He pulled next to the woman. The girls watched her finish putting on mascara and begin applying lipstick.

The scouts were making good time, partly due to the fact they were driving in the carpool lane. However, they were forced to slow down when they caught up with a pickup truck piled high with mattresses driving forty miles an hour.

Rebecca pointed out the front window, "That man is a piggy for driving slowly in the carpool lane with a truck full of mattresses."

"Way to go, Rebecca. You girls would make excellent Piggy Patrol Officers," commented Mr. Hamhock.

By the time the scouts arrived at the campground, they had spotted three more piggies: a smog spewing Suburban, a guy dumping garbage on the side of the road, and a farmer driving a tractor so slowly there were twenty cars lined up behind him, waiting to pass.

However, when Virginia's dad and the scouts pulled into their campsite, they saw evidence of the biggest piggies…

A Messy Campsite

The campsite was a mess. It had been trashed by the previous campers and looked nothing like what Virginia had imagined. She had expected a lush green meadow with a babbling brook running through the middle.

She'd envisioned tall pine trees, with room between to hang the hammock her father bought at the army supply store. She imagined plenty of shade, and the sound of leaves rustling as a gentle breeze blew through the treetops.

Instead, the campsite was a wreck! Mr. Hamhock and the girls got out of the minivan to survey the damage. There were empty cans and garbage strewn across the ground. The fire pit rocks had been moved, and there were half burnt logs lying everywhere. Bread bags, empty pudding cups and used plastic forks littered the trees. It looked as though a tornado had ripped through the campsite just before the scouts arrived.

Obviously, the previous campers had never heard the motto, "Leave the campsite cleaner than you found it." Mr. Hamhock had never seen such a messy campsite.

"This really grinds my gears," said Mr. Hamhock as he looked around. "The previous campers were complete piggies. They should have cleaned up their mess before leaving. This is the worst piggy behavior we've seen all morning."

The scouts nodded in agreement.

He continued, "If I knew who did this, I'd give them a Piggy Ticket so fast it would make their head spin."

"We should clean up so we can start earning badges," said Virginia.

"Oh no. We're not cleaning up this mess. Get back in the van girls. We're going to talk to the Ranger and demand another campsite."

Olivia remarked, "It looked pretty crowded as we drove in. I don't think there are any empty campsites, Mr. Hamhock."

"We'll see about that," he said, heading for the minivan. The girls looked at each other. None of them wanted to leave.

Virginia spoke up, "We're tired of riding in the van. Can we wait here?"

"Suit yourself," said her dad. He started the engine and put the van in reverse.

As Mr. Hamhock backed up, the trailer jacked hard to the left. It was obvious that Virginia's dad was out of his element.

The trailer swerved farther left and the wheel stopped against a log. Virginia's dad gunned the engine. Beyond the log was another campsite. The trailer wheel popped over the log and Mr. Hamhock kept backing up, unaware that the trailer inched closer to the campsite.

The girls watched Mr. Hamhock's progress with a combination of fear and surprise. If he kept backing up he would hit the neighbor's campsite.

Virginia called, "Watch out!"

Mr. Hamhock couldn't hear because the windows were all closed.

He continued backing up. The trailer smacked a folding table, knocking all of the camper's supplies to the ground.

Virginia tried to get her father's attention by waving her hands, but he was intent on backing up and didn't see her. The scouts watched as the trailer pushed the table and chairs into the camper's tent. The tent collapsed.

Mr. Hamhock was oblivious of the damage that the trailer caused. He put the van into drive and pulled forward, trying to straighten the trailer. It was no use.

The girls stared at their neighbor's campsite. The trailer had knocked over the folding table, chairs and tent. Food was scattered all over the ground.

Mr. Hamhock parked the minivan, defeated by the trailer. He got out and smiled nervously, "On second thought, maybe we should just stay here. You girls clean up while I unload the trailer."

Virginia's friends shot her a look. Should they say something about the neighbor's campsite? Virginia decided to let it go and replied, "Okay, Dad." The trailer/campsite incident was better left alone.

The girls spread out around the campsite and began cleaning. Virginia and Rebecca rolled the rocks back to the fire pit. Some of the large stones required both girls working as a team. They arranged the rocks in a circle and stacked the half burnt logs nearby for later use.

Meanwhile, Virginia's dad struggled to unload the trailer. He had packed everything so tightly that he was having trouble unloading the gear. The folding camp cot was stuck between the five-gallon water container and the portable shower. Mr. Hamhock tugged on the cot. He pulled on the cot. He wiggled it back and forth. Finally, it popped out.

Back at the campsite, Franny and Brianna picked trash off the ground. They collected empty tin cans, eggshells and a deflated beach ball. The previous campers really were piggies. The girls couldn't believe anyone would leave so much trash at a campsite. Franny and Brianna piled the garbage up. Soon, they realized they needed a garbage can.

Mr. Hamhock had unloaded half of the trailer when Franny and Brianna approached.

"We're making progress with the campsite cleanup. Do you have any garbage bags?" asked Franny.

"Of course I have garbage bags," replied Mr. Hamhock. He searched through the pile of camping supplies stacked next to the trailer. "Garbage bags, garbage bags," he repeated, continuing the search. "Garbage bags should be with the food supplies."

Virginia's dad rooted through the camping gear. "We've got a folding shovel and emergency space blankets. Where are the garbage bags? We have a case of biodegradable toilet paper and a signal mirror, but I can't find the garbage bags."

Franny and Brianna wondered if Mr. Hamhock had forgotten to buy garbage bags.

He suggested, "Maybe you can just pile the trash up."

Franny countered, "The wind might blow the trash around the campground." She looked at the camping gear and noticed the packages of space blankets. "Could we borrow some of those space blankets and some rope?"

"No problem. Take whatever you need," said Mr. Hamhock as he returned to the trailer.

Franny grabbed three of the space blankets. Brianna picked up a small spool of rope and asked, "Do you have any scissors?"

"I've got something better than scissors," said Mr. Hamhock, smiling.

He pulled a knife out of his pocket. It was the knife his grandfather had given him. He flicked the blade open and unwound a length of rope from the spool. "How much rope do you need?"

Franny responded, "Three pieces about this long." She motion with her hands.

He cut the rope and handed the pieces to Franny.

"Thanks, Mr. Hamhock."

"You're welcome, Franny."

Brianna and Franny headed back to the campsite with the space blankets and rope. Mr. Hamhock continued unloading the trailer. Next was the largest item that he'd packed. It was a Barcalounger, his favorite chair. This was no ordinary chair. It was the most comfortable chair ever made. The Barcalounger swiveled around. There was a lever on the side that made the chair recline, making it perfect for a nap.

Unfortunately, the rest of the family didn't share Mr. Hamhock's love of the Barcalounger. Mrs. Hamhock thought it was ugly. After they redecorated the family room, she banished the Barcalounger to the garage. It had been months since Mr. Hamhock sat in his chair, so he packed it in the trailer for the camping trip.

He struggled to drag the Barcalounger from the trailer. It took him nearly ten minutes of heavy lifting. After successfully unloading the chair, Mr. Hamhock was dripping with sweat and breathing heavily. He sat down in his favorite chair for a break.

Lacey and Olivia were taller than the other girls, so they volunteered for tree cleaning duty. They plucked plastic forks from branches and untangled plastic bags from bushes. After amassing a large collection of garbage, Lacey and Olivia piled their trash in the middle of the campsite.

Franny and Brianna unfolded one of the space blankets and spread it out on the ground. They loaded their trash on the space blanket, gathered the corners together and tied the whole thing up with a piece of rope. Voilà, instant garbage bag.

Following Franny and Brianna's lead, the other girls wrapped their trash into makeshift garbage bags. Soon, there were three neatly packed bags of trash sitting in the middle of the campsite.

Virginia looked around. The campsite, which had been a horrible mess, looked beautiful now that the girls had finished their cleanup.

There was plenty of shade from the beautiful trees that were previously covered with forks and pudding cups. The fire pit was ready for a crackling campfire, and there was a small creek beyond the grassy meadow where the girls would pitch their tent.

The girls gave each other a series of high fives and headed to tell Mr. Hamhock they were ready to start earning badges.

They found Virginia's father curled up in his Barcalounger, fast asleep!

Pitching the Tent

Mr. Hamhock was sleeping so deeply that he was snoring. The girls looked at each other, unsure what to do. Finally, Virginia realized it was up to her to wake her father from his nap. She gently shook his shoulder. Nothing. She shook his shoulder a little harder. Her father gave a snort. She jumped back, startled. The other girls laughed.

Virginia shook her father's shoulder a third time and called, "Dad, time to wake up!"

Her father woke from his slumber. He looked up at the girls. It took him a moment to realize where he was.

Mr. Hamhock hopped out of his Barcalounger,

embarrassed that he'd fallen asleep. "I was just checking to make sure my chair still works. Yep. It still reclines," he joked.

"We finished cleaning up the campsite," said Olivia.

Brianna added, "We're ready to start earning our badges."

Mr. Hamhock responded, "Whoa, Nelly. We can't start working on badges until we've set up camp. That's the first rule of camping. Always set up camp first. Then you're prepared for the rest of the day."

He pulled a stuff sack from the trailer and handed it to Virginia. "Here's your tent. You go pitch it while I finish unloading the trailer."

"We've never pitched a tent before," she protested.

"It's easy. Everything's in that bag. Tent, poles and stakes. You'll see," her father responded.

Virginia and the other scouts headed back to the grassy meadow with the tent. Mr. Hamhock pulled a folding table and a stack of camp chairs out of the trailer.

Meanwhile, the girls opened the stuff sack and unrolled the tent. There was a stack of poles and a handful of stakes rolled up inside. Not knowing where to begin, the girls spread out around the tent. Virginia and Rebecca tried to prop the tent up with several poles, but the poles weren't tall enough.

A vehicle pulled into the campsite. It was a Forest Service truck. The door opened and a Ranger got out. He was dressed in khaki and wore a ranger's hat with a US Forest Service patch on the front.

"Good morning," said the Ranger as he approached. The girls stopped working on the tent.

Franny responded, "Hello."

"Is there a grownup around?" the Ranger asked.

Virginia pointed to the minivan, "My dad is unloading the trailer." She called out, "Dad. There's a Park Ranger to see you."

Mr. Hamhock appeared from behind the minivan and greeted the Ranger with a handshake, "I'm Hank Hamhock. What can I do for you?"

"Bob," the Ranger said. "I wanted to stop by and alert you about a situation. Looks like your neighbor had a little catastrophe at their campsite."

The scouts gave each other a knowing look. They knew the cause of the damage… Virginia's dad.

Ranger Bob continued, "Something trashed their campsite, rooted through their food and knocked over their tent."

"Wow," commented Mr. Hamhock, "Are the

46

campers okay?"

Ranger Bob responded, "Thankfully, yes. They were out hiking when it happened. But, I wanted to stop by and warn you because it was probably a wild bear."

"A wild bear?" exclaimed Virginia's dad. He turned to the scouts, "You girls pack up your stuff. If there's a wild bear on the loose, we're getting the heck out of here."

The girls shot each other a nervous glance. Should they tell Ranger Bob that Mr. Hamhock had destroyed their neighbors' campsite?

"There's no reason to be alarmed," said Ranger Bob. "There hasn't been a bear in this area for years. He probably just smelled some food that was left out on their table."

Mr. Hamhock looked concerned, "Are you sure? It would be terrible if one of my scouts was eaten by a wild bear!"

Ranger Bob continued, "No one is going to be eaten by a bear. You simply need to exercise caution with your food supplies. I would suggest that you make a bear bag."

"A bear bag?" asked Mr. Hamhock.

"Load all of your food into a bag and hang it from a tree branch with some rope. You should be fine."

Virginia's dad nervously assured the girls, "You hear that girls? Everything will be okay if we take the right precautions."

Ranger Bob noticed the tent pieces lying on the ground. "You girls need help pitching that tent? They can be a little tricky."

Brianna responded, "Thank you. That would be..."

"...Unnecessary," interrupted Mr. Hamhock. "We've got it covered. Thanks for offering."

"Alright," continued Ranger Bob. "If you have any questions, I'll be in the Ranger Station at the entrance to the campground. You all have a nice day." He got in his truck and drove away.

Mr. Hamhock started back toward the trailer. Virginia looked at the tent, "Dad, we can't figure out how to pitch the tent. Can you help us?"

"Of course," said her dad. "First, you have to organize the parts. We've got the tent, poles and stakes." He separated the parts into different piles.

He pointed to the corners of the tent, "You girls grab the other corners and spread the tent out on a flat area of ground." Olivia, Lacey, Brianna and Franny each grabbed a corner of the tent and laid it out on the grass.

Mr. Hamhock continued, "Now, pull the corners and put a stake into the ground to keep it tight." He tossed a stake to each of the girls.

Virginia watched her dad and smiled. She was proud that he knew so much about camping.

"Now we use the poles to support the tent at each end," her dad continued. He grabbed a pole and tried to support the tent, but the pole was too short. Adding another section made the pole too long. A puzzled expression spread across his face.

He grabbed another pole from the pile. It was also too short. Virginia's dad stepped back for a moment to analyze the situation. His snout twitched as he compared the poles. They were all different lengths. Maybe they were supposed to fit together...

Mr. Hamhock connected several of the pole pieces and approached the tent, "Okay girls, hold the ends up. I think this pole supports the tent from the inside."

Virginia commented, "Dad, I think the poles go in these sleeves on the outside." She pointed to several nylon sleeves on the outside of the tent.

Her father objected, "These poles are too long for those sleeves. Hold the tent up so I can get inside."

Virginia held up her end of the tent. Mr. Hamhock crawled inside with the pole.

The girls watched as Virginia's father stood up inside the tent. He stuck one end of the pole into the bottom corner of the tent. The other end pushed against the top of the tent, flexing against the nylon material.

"I need another pole piece," called Mr. Hamhock.

Lacey handed another section through the door of the tent.

Mr. Hamhock bent the pole so it would fit inside the tent. The nylon fabric stretched as he struggled with the pole.

"I've… almost… got it…" Virginia's dad called from inside the tent.

Suddenly, there was a loud SNAP, followed by RRRRIIIIIIIPPPPPP!

A piece of the broken pole shot through the nylon material and almost hit Virginia in the face. Her father tried to pull the pole back into the tent, but the pole slid sideways, ripping a hole the length of the tent.

The nylon fabric fell away to reveal Virginia's father holding both ends of the broken pole. He was red with embarrassment and stammered, "These poles are the wrong size. They must have gotten switched last time this tent was used." He chucked the poles aside and stepped through the hole.

Lacey asked, "Do you have any tape Mr. Hamhock? We can probably patch the hole. My daddy always says, 'duct tape can fix anything'."

"Brilliant idea, Lacey. Of course I've got duct tape. What kind of a woodsman would I be without a roll of duct tape?" He headed to the minivan to retrieve the tape, leaving the girls standing next to the tent.

"Sorry," Virginia apologized to the other girls.

"Nothing a little duct tape can't fix," replied Lacey.

"He was just trying to help," added Rebecca trying to make her best friend feel better.

Mr. Hamhock returned with a roll of duct tape, "We'll have that tent patched in no time. Olivia, Lacey and Brianna, you spread the side of the tent out so we can see the whole hole. Virginia, you grab the end of the tape. On three, pull the tape the entire length of the rip. Franny and Rebecca, you guide the tape onto the rip so that it seals the hole.

"Ready everyone?" The girls nodded. Mr. Hamhock held out the roll of duct tape. Virginia grabbed the loose end. He counted, "One, two, three!" Virginia pulled the end of the tape, expecting it to unfurl five feet to match the rip. Instead, several inches of tape peeled from the roll, and then a foot of brown paper peeled away. The roll was out of tape, and the scouts were out of luck.

"Oh for crying out loud!" yelled Mr. Hamhock. "Who used all of my duct tape?" He threw the empty tape roll on the ground and looked at Virginia. "I'll bet it was your little brother, Sammy. I've told him a thousand times to stay out of my toolbox."

Brianna offered, "Who needs a tent anyway? I want to sleep under the stars."

"Yeah," echoed Franny. "I can't wait to see the Big Dipper and Orion's Belt."

Mr. Hamhock's anger faded. He rolled the tent up and asked, "Who's ready for arts and crafts?"

Arts and Crafts

Mr. Hamhock pulled a plastic bin from the trailer and set it on a folding table next to the fire pit. The scouts were seated in camp chairs around the table, ready for their arts and crafts project.

He opened the bin and unloaded the supplies that Brianna's mother had packed for the girls.

There were six pieces of cardboard - four inches tall by six inches wide, a bottle of glue, a roll of twine, a pair of scissors and a box of colored pencils.

Mr. Hamhock began reading the instructions, "How to make twig easels and nature drawings. First, gather a collection of twigs, small pinecones, acorns, leaves and pebbles."

"Break three twigs about ten inches long and a fourth twig about seven inches long."

"Glue two of the long twigs together and add the short twig to form an A shape."

He held up the instructions that showed an illustration.

"Tie the joints with twine so that they hold. Add a little more glue."

"Glue the third long twig to the A shape, forming an easel. Tie the joint with twine."

"While the glue is drying on your easel, use some colored pencils to draw a picture on the cardboard. You can draw whatever you want: a landscape, the clouds in the sky or a sunset."

"After you've finished your drawing, use your collection of nature treasures to make a frame around your art piece."

"Glue twigs, acorns, small leaves and pebbles onto the cardboard in the shape of a frame."

"Rest the framed drawing on your easel for a piece of art that will remind you of your campout."

Mr. Hamhock asked, "Any questions?"

The girls shook their heads. They were anxious to start on the project. He set the instructions on the table and said, "You girls get started. I'm going to finish unloading the trailer."

The girls jumped up from the table and spread out around the campsite, collecting bits of nature for their arts and crafts project.

Lacey found some sticks with white bark on the outside. Olivia broke several twigs from a branch. There were still leaves attached. Franny climbed up a tree and found some green acorns she thought would look good on her frame.

Mr. Hamhock opened a popup shade tent and adjusted the height so that he could stand underneath without bumping his head.

Rebecca searched the creek and found a rock with a small hole worn through it. Virginia discovered a plant with leaves that felt like a lamb's ear.

At the trailer, Virginia's dad unpacked a small generator. He plugged a power strip into the generator. Then he plugged his cell phone charger into the power strip.

Brianna sat beneath a large tree reading her book. The breeze blew through the trees, and a small pinecone landed in her lap. She looked at the ground and noticed that it was covered with hundreds of pinecones and sticks. She scooped up a handful of the earthen treasures and carried them back to the table.

Mr. Hamhock plugged an extension cord into the power strip. The cord ran to a square object covered with a furniture pad. He pulled the pad off to reveal a television.

The girls gathered at the table and began assembling their easels. After breaking the sticks to the proper lengths, they used glue and twine to hold the joints together.

Virginia's dad unfolded a ladder and fastened a clamp to the top step. He opened a cardboard box and pulled out a satellite dish. The satellite dish fastened to the clamp on the ladder and pointed at the sky. Mr. Hamhock looked at his watch and smiled.

While the easels dried, each of the scouts grabbed a piece of cardboard and a handful of colored pencils. They separated and found quiet spots to draw their favorite views of the campsite.

Virginia imagined a roaring campfire in the fire pit. She used red, orange and yellow pencils to draw a glowing night scene.

Franny lay on her back and looked up at the treetops swaying against the blue sky. She used green and blue pencils to draw the leaves and sky.

Brianna fell in love with a knothole in a large oak tree and decided to draw a close up.

Virginia's dad pulled the handle on the generator. It hummed to life. He flicked the power button on the power strip. The light glowed orange. Mr. Hamhock flopped into his Barcalounger and grabbed the remote.

Rebecca took a walk down to the creek and drew a waterscape with blue and gray pencils.

Olivia imagined droplets of morning dew on the grass next to the fire pit. She sketched an early morning scene with rays of sunlight pouring through the trees.

Lacey wondered what the campsite would look like covered in snow. She drew a stark landscape with bare branches and snowdrifts against the tree trunks.

The girls gathered back at the table and compared drawings. They spread out their forest treasures and glued them on the edge of the cardboard to create frames around their illustrations.

Virginia stood her easel up on the table. She placed her drawing on the easel and smiled, "One badge down. Seven to go!"

Suddenly, a noise pierced the calm of the woods. It sounded like cheering. Then a man began speaking. The voice sounded like it was coming from a loudspeaker. It echoed through the woods.

The girls got up from the table. They gravitated toward the sound, which was coming from behind the minivan.

When the girls peeked around the minivan, they saw that Virginia's dad was sitting in his Barcalounger, watching a baseball game on television. One of the players hit the ball and Mr. Hamhock let out a whoop of excitement.

"Dad, what are you doing?" Virginia asked. She couldn't believe he had brought a television on the campout.

Her dad looked up, "Uh, I'm watching the ballgame."

"We're supposed to be camping."

"I couldn't miss the game," he protested.

Campers at the neighboring sites were not happy about the noise. They looked angry and annoyed. Virginia realized she had to act quickly, before the other campers ran them out of the campground.

"We're finished with our arts and crafts project," she said.

Her dad pleaded, "Let me just watch one inning."

Virginia commanded, "C'mon, Dad. We're ready to go on a hike."

63

Mr. Hamhock struggled out of his Barcalounger, "I guess I can save it on my DVR." He pressed several buttons on the remote. The television turned off and the woods were silent again.

He looked at the girls and said, "Grab your water bottles, we're going for a hike!"

A Hike in the Woods

Mr. Hamhock and the scouts followed a hiking trail out of their campsite. They walked next to the babbling brook for a half-mile, then the trail crossed to the other side. A huge tree trunk spanned the brook from bank to bank, creating a bridge for hikers.

"Log bridges can be tricky," Virginia's dad cautioned as he tested the log with his foot to make sure it was secure. "The main thing is for everyone to make it across without falling in the water. It doesn't matter how you get to the other side. You can sit on the log and scooch across on your butt. You can do somersaults for all I care. Just don't fall in. Okay?"

The girls nodded. Virginia looked down at the water flowing under the log, gurgling and bubbling as it rushed past. The creek was only several inches deep so there was no chance of drowning. Falling off the log would be more embarrassing than dangerous.

Her dad stepped out on the log and extended his arms. "It helps to use your arms for balance," he said, quickly stepping across the log bridge safely to the other bank. Virginia smiled, proud that he made the bridge crossing look so easy.

Ten minutes later, all of the girls were safe and sound on the opposite bank of the creek. No one fell into the water. They were ready to continue their hike.

A furry animal popped up on a rock and stared at the scouts. It was about the size of a rolled up sleeping bag. Lacey saw the animal and shrieked, "Look out, there's a bear."

The other girls turned to look at the animal.

Franny said, "I don't think that's a bear. It's too small."

"It looks like it could be a squirrel," Virginia added.

Olivia shook her head, "It's too big for a squirrel."

Brianna said, "I think it's a marmot."

The marmot stood up on its hind legs. Its tail twitched nervously as it tried to determine if the scouts were friend or foe.

"He's so cute," squealed Virginia. "Can I feed him?"

"No," snapped her dad. "That animal might carry rabies or some other disease."

A moment later, the marmot darted into the woods.

Mr. Hamhock spoke, "I don't want you girls to worry about wild animals. The bear that destroyed our neighbor's campsite is probably miles away by now." He looked nervously around the woods, as if searching for signs of wildlife.

The scouts shared a knowing glance. They weren't worried about wild animals, especially bears. They knew that the attack on their neighbors' campsite was really Mr. Hamhock.

Virginia's dad continued speaking, louder than necessary, "We won't have any trouble if we make plenty of noise while we walk." He picked up a long stick and began beating bushes to scare away any wild animals that might be hiding nearby.

The trail followed the creek through a forest of large trees swaying in the breeze. "These are oak trees," explained Mr. Hamhock as they walked under the canopy of green. He picked a leaf off the ground and held it up for the girls to see. "In the fall, these leaves will turn different colors of red, yellow and orange."

The trail turned left and headed uphill. Hiking became more strenuous. The girls plodded up the incline as the trail zigzagged higher.

Olivia whined, "How come this trail keeps winding back and forth?"

Mr. Hamhock explained, "These are called switchbacks. The hill is so steep that we could never hike straight up. The trailblazers cut a zigzag pattern to make hiking less difficult. Let's keep walking at an even pace as we head uphill. Before you know it, we'll be at the top."

When the trail leveled out, the scouts stopped for a break. "Who's hungry?" asked Virginia's dad as he pulled lunch out of his daypack.

"I'm starving," said Lacey.

"Me too," echoed Olivia.

Virginia's dad spread lunch out for the girls. There was a large un-sliced loaf of bread, a wedge of cheese, a package of beef jerky, a bag of carrots, a bag of celery sticks, a bag of trail mix and several boxes of scout cookies.

Mr. Hamhock pulled his pocketknife out and wiped the blade on his jeans to clean it.

He sawed the bread into slices, and cut the wedge of cheese into chunks. The girls devoured the bread and cheese within minutes.

The scouts passed on the carrots, celery, beef jerky and trail mix. What they really wanted was cookies. Olivia, Lacey and Brianna loved Do-si-dos. Thin Mints were the favorite of Franny, Rebecca and Virginia. Mr. Hamhock liked Samoas.

As the girls munched on scout cookies, they heard a noise. It sounded like something moving through the woods. Mr. Hamhock jumped up, holding his stick like a spear.

The noise got louder. Mr. Hamhock yelled, "I have a weapon, and I'm not afraid to use it. We don't want any trouble, so just move along." He and the girls scanned the woods for movement, but saw nothing.

The breeze blew overhead and the noise became louder still, screeching like a monkey. Suddenly, a large branch from an old oak tree cracked and crashed to the ground several yards away from the girls.

Mr. Hamhock and the girls were relieved that they weren't being attacked by a wild bear.

The beef jerky, carrots, celery and trail mix sat untouched on the daypack while the scouts washed down their cookies with several swigs of water.

After packing up their lunch leftovers, the scouts hit the trail and continued upwards. The oak trees thinned out as the woods opened to reveal a grassy meadow dotted with thousands of wildflowers.

One of the scout trips was to a greenhouse. The girls had met a flower expert, known as a horticulturalist, who showed them a variety of wildflowers.

In the meadow, Olivia recognized a flower called the Black- Eyed Susan. It was bright yellow with long petals and a dark button eye in the middle.

Brianna pointed to a cluster of Forget-Me-Not flowers. They were small, bright blue and shaped like a star.

Up ahead, the meadow looked like it was covered with snow. When the girls got closer, they realized that the meadow was covered with thousands of dandelions. The white seed heads stuck up from patches of green leaves.

The scouts each grabbed a stalk and blew the seeds. Hundreds of seeds floated in the air.

Mr. Hamhock plucked a seed head from a plant and said, "Legend has it that blowing the seeds off a dandelion is said to carry your thoughts and dreams to a loved one." He blew the seeds off his dandelion. The breeze carried the seeds high across the meadow. "Go little seeds. Tell Mrs. Hamhock that I love her."

The scouts giggled. Virginia rolled her eyes, embarrassed.

"I read that you can eat dandelion leaves," offered Brianna. "Is that true, Mr. Hamhock?"

"You sure can, Brianna," replied Virginia's dad as he plucked a dandelion leaf and popped it in his mouth.

"Yuck," responded Olivia.

"I'd have to be pretty hungry to eat dandelion leaves," said Lacey.

Mr. Hamhock said, "It's good to know which plants are edible, just in case."

Brianna took a small bite of a dandelion leaf and chewed it. "Not bad," she said.

The scouts and Mr. Hamhock resumed hiking. Beyond the Dandelions was a sea of orange and yellow, made up of gorgeous flowers called Indian Blankets. They were round with a brown center and bright orange petals tipped with yellow, as though they'd been dipped in paint.

As the girls continued through the field of

flowers, Virginia's father stopped to watch some butterflies flitting from flower to flower, collecting pollen.

It wasn't long before the girls crossed the meadow. They headed into a forest of giant pine trees. Virginia's father fell farther behind, but the girls didn't notice. They were too busy looking at the shafts of sunlight filtering through the tree branches.

In the distance, a noise pierced the silence of the woods. It sounded like a jackhammer slamming against a tree trunk. The girls realized that they were hearing a woodpecker. As they continued down the trail, the sound got louder.

The scouts rounded a bend and saw a hiker standing next to a camera on a tripod. As the girls approached, the hiker put his finger to his lips, motioning them to be quiet.

"I just spotted a Pileated Woodpecker," he whispered. "It's a very rare bird and I'm trying to get a photo."

The scouts approached the hiker, careful to avoid stepping on sticks that might make noise. He pointed upwards, "It's in that tree." The girls looked, but they couldn't see anything. The pecking noise started again, filling the woods with sound. Then it stopped. The girls saw a flash of red halfway up the tree.

The hiker was excited, "Did you see it? That beautiful red head?" The girls grinned. They had seen it. The hiker looked through the lens of his camera, "C'mon fella. Poke your head around so I can get a picture."

There was a hint of black sticking out from behind the tree trunk. The girls watched anxiously as the woodpecker moved a little farther around. Now they could see white feathers on the bird's neck. The hiker stared through his camera lens, "Just a little farther and I can get the perfect shot."

The woodpecker moved even farther around the trunk. Now the girls could see a sliver of the bird's red head. None of them had ever seen a woodpecker before and this was a Pileated Woodpecker, the rarest of woodpeckers.

Just as the woodpecker moved into view, a voice pierced the air. "VIRGINIA!" It was Virginia's father, yelling her name as he pounded through the woods, hitting bushes with his stick to frighten away wild animals. "VIRGINIA!" he shouted again.

Startled, the Pileated Woodpecker popped off the tree and flew away. "VIRGINIA!" shouted Mr. Hamhock, closer now. The hiker looked up from his camera. His shoulders dropped in disappointment. The woodpecker had flown before he could snap a photo. Frustrated, he jerked his camera off the tripod.

Realizing the moment was spoiled, Virginia answered, "Over here, Dad."

Mr. Hamhock stopped next the girls, "Where have you been? I was worried that you'd been attacked."

"We were bird watching," replied Virginia.

"We saw a Pileated Woodpecker," added Brianna. "It's a very rare bird."

"And I didn't get a photo!" yelled the hiker. He picked up his tripod and stormed away.

Mr. Hamhock watched the hiker disappear around the bend and commented, "That hiker wasn't very friendly."

The girls looked at each other. None of them felt like telling Virginia's father that he was to blame.

Mr. Hamhock said, "We should head back to camp. We'll need to start fixing dinner soon."

Lacey exclaimed, "Dinner? But we just ate lunch."

Mr. Hamhock replied, "Trust me, you'll be hungry by the time we get back to camp."

Dinner Time

Mr. Hamhock was right. By the time the scouts arrived back at their campsite, they had walked so far that they were starving.

"In order to cook dinner, we need to build a fire," announced Virginia's dad. "And to make a fire, we'll need firewood. The first girl who delivers two armfuls of wood gets to light the fire."

While the girls scoured the woods for firewood, Mr. Hamhock unpacked the food bags from the trailer and spread the fixings out on the table near the fire pit. The menu consisted of spaghetti with meat sauce and garlic bread.

Out of the first food bag came fresh tomatoes,

onions, garlic and two pounds of ground beef. Out of a second bag came three large loaves of French bread, several sticks of butter and a container of garlic powder.

Franny, Rebecca and Olivia each returned with their first load of firewood. Mr. Hamhock pointed to a spot next to the fire pit, "Good job girls. You can pile the wood right there." The three girls dropped their wood next to the fire pit and took off for another armful as Virginia and Lacey appeared with their first load.

Mr. Hamhock organized the cooking gear as Virginia and Lacey dumped their armfuls of wood onto the growing pile. As they returned to the woods, he unpacked the nesting pots, cutting boards and knives.

Brianna darted out of the woods with an armload of freshly cut saplings that looked as though they had just been gnawed by her sharp beaver teeth. She asked, "Where should I put these, Mr. Hamhock?"

He looked at the newly cut wood. It was too green to burn, but he refrained from scolding Brianna. She had worked hard to deliver her first armload. He pointed to a spot near the fire pit, "Dump it next to that pile of logs, Brianna. For your second load, try to find some old dry wood lying on the ground."

Brianna looked up with a smile and responded, "Okay." She disappeared into the woods for another load.

As Virginia's dad finished organizing the cooking gear, Franny ran out of the woods with her second armload. Rebecca was close behind.

Franny dumped her wood onto the pile and thrust her arms into the air.

"We have a winner!" yelled Mr. Hamhock.

Franny did a victory dance around the fire pit as the rest of the girls appeared with their second loads of wood.

"Alright girls, gather round. I'm going to show you how to build a fire," said Mr. Hamhock as he stepped near the pile of firewood. He grabbed a bundle of small sticks and a handful of pine needles. The girls surrounded the fire pit and watched as he knelt down and began to arrange the sticks.

"There are two ways you can start a fire. First, you can make a lean-to." Mr. Hamhock rested several sticks against a small log, forming a lean-to. He stuffed a handful of pine needles underneath. "Pine needles make perfect kindling."

Virginia's dad motioned to the finished lean-to and looked at the girls to make sure they were paying attention.

He grabbed another handful of sticks, "The second way you can start a fire is with a stick tepee." Mr. Hamhock stuck several sticks in the ground and leaned them together to form a tepee. He stuffed a handful of pine needles underneath, and leaned more sticks around the outside of the tepee. "Personally, the tepee is my favorite way to start a fire."

He turned to Franny and asked, "Are you ready to light the fire?"

Franny nodded nervously. Mr. Hamhock pulled a box of matches out of his pocket. Franny stepped forward. He handed her the matches and instructed, "Kneel down next to the fire pit, strike a match against the side of the box and hold it under the pine needles until they catch fire."

Franny followed Mr. Hamhock's instructions. She lit the pine needles under the tepee, and then lit the pine needles under the lean-to. In moments, the pine needles ignited. Then, some of the sticks caught. Soon, the teepee and lean-to were engulfed in flames. The other girls cheered.

Virginia's dad set several small logs on top of the flames, "We'll keep adding larger logs until the fire is big enough to cook dinner. While that's happening, let's prep the ingredients. Who wants to chop vegetables?"

Six hands shot up. Everyone wanted to help. Mr. Hamhock walked to the table where all of the dinner fixings were spread out.

"Olivia, you chop these onions into little pieces," he said, handing Olivia a knife and a chopping board. "Brianna, you're on garlic duty. Franny, you cut up these peppers," he said, handing each of the girls a knife.

Suddenly, there was a loud POP from the campfire. A small log exploded, sending cinders out past the rocks of the fire pit. The logs on top of the campfire shifted from the force of the explosion.

"What was that?" exclaimed Lacey.

"Don't worry, it's just a log popping. Sometimes there's moisture trapped in a piece of wood. As the moisture heats, steam builds inside. That popping noise was the sound of steam escaping," said Mr. Hamhock as he stomped the burning cinders with the heel of his boot.

"That's why fires are so dangerous," commented Lacey.

"That's right, Lacey."

He walked back to the table. Virginia, Rebecca and Lacey waited patiently for their assignments. Mr. Hamhock pointed to the bread, butter and garlic powder. "You girls are going to make garlic bread. Virginia, you're the slicer. Rebecca, you're the butterer. Lacey, you're the sprinkler. When the loaves are ready, wrap them in tin foil and we'll toast them on the fire."

With the girls busy, Virginia's father tended to the fire. He set several large logs on top. The flames grew higher. Virginia asked, "Dad, don't you think the fire is big enough?"

"You're talking to a master fire builder," he responded. "We need a nice big flame to boil water." He chucked another large log on the fire and gave Virginia a thumbs up.

Mr. Hamhock filled the largest pot with water and lugged it to the fire pit. He struggled to lift the pot and carefully set it on top of several logs, in the middle of the flames. He put the lid on and stepped back to the table.

Next was the ground beef. Virginia's dad put the meat in a frying pan. He rested the pan on another log in the fire. The meat began to sizzle as the flames heated the pan.

Mr. Hamhock asked, "How's the chopping?"

The girls looked up from their chopping boards and smiled. That is, except Olivia. Her eyes were tearing from the onions.

Franny answered, "We're just about finished."

"Great," grinned Mr. Hamhock. "Dump the onions, peppers and garlic into a pot with some oil and we'll put it on the fire."

The garlic bread girls were like factory workers on an assembly line. Virginia sliced the bread, Rebecca spread the butter and Lacey sprinkled the garlic powder. After Virginia sliced the last loaf, she began to wrap the finished pieces in tin foil.

Her father opened the top of the water pot and dumped two boxes of spaghetti into the boiling water. The veggie girls finished chopping. Mr. Hamhock grabbed the vegetable pot and set it on the fire. He placed the tin foil wrapped loaves of garlic bread on the coals.

"Cooking on a campfire is like juggling," said Virginia's dad as he added a can of tomato sauce to the frying pan. "You have to keep an eye on each pot so it doesn't burn." He added another log to the fire and stepped back to admire his handy work.

"It'll be a few minutes before dinner is ready. Perfect time to relax while everything cooks."

Virginia's dad grabbed a stick and plopped down on a log near the fire pit. He opened his pocketknife and began to whittle.

Lacey suggested, "Let's work on our arts and crafts project." The other girls agreed. Franny and

Olivia finished their drawings. Lacey and Rebecca added details to their frames. Virginia tied more twine around the joints of her easel. Brianna opened her book and continued reading.

What a perfect time of day. The setting sun cast an orange glow around the campsite. Birds chirped as they flitted from tree to tree. The fire crackled and the pasta water bubbled. Soon, dinner would be ready. The girls were starving from their strenuous hike up the mountain.

A log on the fire began to hiss. The girls knew that the sound was caused by moisture trapped inside the log. The hiss turned to a whistling sound. The girls looked at each other and giggled. Then, there was a huge POP and a shower of cinders exploded from the log as the steam escaped. Mr. Hamhock jumped up from his log and stomped the burning cinders into the dirt with the heel of his boot.

Several logs on the fire shifted. All eyes looked at the fire pit as the pasta pot leaned slightly. Water sloshed over the side of the pot and sizzled on the hot coals.

The logs shifted again. As if in slow motion, the pasta pot leaned further. Mr. Hamhock turned toward the fire pit, but before he could react, the pasta pot tipped sideways. Boiling water and pasta cascaded onto the bubbling meat sauce in the frying pan. The pasta pot bumped the vegetable pot, knocking it over, spilling the vegetables onto the sizzling logs.

By the time Mr. Hamhock pulled the garlic bread from the smoldering embers, the bread was soaked with water from the pasta pot.

The girls looked at the fire pit in disbelief. With one pop, their entire dinner had been ruined.

"That's the first time I've ever seen that happen," said Mr. Hamhock. He looked at the table and stated the obvious. "Looks like we're out of dinner fixings."

Virginia's stomach rumbled.

Brianna looked at the smoking fire pit and asked, "What are we going to eat?"

Mr. Hamhock shrugged, "I don't know."

Lacey pulled a granola bar out of her pocket and laid it on the table, "My mom gave me this granola bar in case I got hungry. I'll share."

"That's thoughtful, Lacey," said Virginia's dad. "But it's not enough for everyone. We're going to need something else to eat."

"What about the leftover carrots and celery sticks from lunch?" asked Olivia.

"And the beef jerky," added Rebecca.

Franny looked down at the pasta pot, "There's still some pasta left in the pot."

Virginia had an idea. She suggested, "What if we make a pot of soup? We could use the beef jerky for flavoring, and add the carrots, celery and what's left of the pasta."

Brianna offered, "We could make a salad out of dandelion leaves and trail mix."

"Brilliant!" said Virginia's dad as he rifled through his knapsack. He piled the leftover lunch supplies on the table, "Let's get to work."

The scouts snapped into action. Olivia chopped the celery sticks. Lacey diced the carrots. Rebecca sliced the beef jerky.

Franny salvaged the remaining pasta into a clean pot. Brianna scoured the campsite for dandelion leaves, and Virginia helped her father rebuild a smaller fire.

Forty minutes later, the scouts were eating dandelion salad and "Log Pop" soup. Their makeshift dinner tasted delicious.

As the sun set below the horizon, the trees surrounding the campsite were silhouetted against a brilliant sky that turned from orange to deep purple. Crickets chirped in the distance, frogs croaked in the creek and the fire crackled.

S'mores and Ghost Stories

Virginia placed a small log on the fire. The bark caught within moments. Flames danced and leapt above the logs, glowing yellow and orange in the darkness of the night.

She sat back down on a log next to Rebecca. It was time to relax and enjoy the evening. Her dad asked, "Who knows a good campfire game we can play?" Rebecca and Lacey raised their hands. He pointed to Lacey and asked, "What's your suggestion?"

"How about telephone?" she asked.

"That's a good one," said Mr. Hamhock. "Why don't you start?"

Lacey thought for a moment and whispered in

Olivia's ear.

Olivia nodded, then she whispered in Brianna's ear. Brianna smiled and turned to Rebecca. After hearing the phrase, Rebecca scrunched up her face, puzzled. The fun of the telephone game had begun. Something in the phrase didn't make sense. Rebecca struggled to figure out what Brianna whispered.

Next, Virginia listened carefully as Rebecca whispered in her ear. Virginia laughed at the absurdity of what she'd heard. The other girls giggled, wondering how the phrase had been transformed. Virginia whispered in Franny's ear.

Franny burst out laughing. The other girls sat on the edge of their logs, waiting patiently to hear how the phrase had been altered as it traveled around the fire.

Mr. Hamhock leaned down and Franny whispered in his ear. A confused look spread across his face as he tried to understand the phrase.

"What did she say?" blurted Brianna.

Olivia chimed in, "Yeah, tell us what you heard!"

The girls leaned forward as Mr. Hamhock started to speak.

"I found a lime in a crate, it was squashed and mixed with flowers" said Mr. Hamhock.

Lacey told everyone, "The phrase started as 'I

like lemonade, but sometimes it tastes sour'."

The girls exploded with laughter.

"That was fun," said Virginia. "What should we do next?"

"Let's make s'mores," suggested Lacey.

"Yeah, s'mores," the other girls chimed in.

"Okay," Mr. Hamhock agreed. "S'mores it is. But first, everyone has to find a long stick to roast marshmallows."

The girls searched the woodpile next to the campfire. Soon, they returned with marshmallow sticks.

Mr. Hamhock pointed at the folding table, "The s'more fixing's are in a grocery bag on the table."

The girls grabbed the grocery bag from the table and brought it back to the campfire. Brianna pulled out a box of graham crackers. Olivia pulled out several chocolate bars. Rebecca reached for the marshmallows, but the grocery bag was empty.

"Where are the marshmallows?" she asked.

"They should be in that bag with the graham crackers and chocolate," replied Mr. Hamhock.

Rebecca held the grocery bag upside down. It was empty.

Brianna panicked, "We can't make s'mores without marshmallows!"

"Don't worry," said Mr. Hamhock. "They're probably in another bag. Why don't you look around the dinner table?"

The girls grabbed their flashlights and searched all of the grocery bags. No luck. They hunted under the table. Still, no luck.

Virginia yelled, "Dad, we can't find the marshmallows. Are you sure you packed them?"

"Of course I packed them," he replied. "You're probably just not looking hard enough."

"We've looked everywhere. We can't find them."

"Alright," he sighed. "I'll come look."

Mr. Hamhock got up from his seat on the log and plodded over to the table. He pointed to a grocery bag and asked, "Did you look in there?"

"Uh huh," replied Rebecca. "No marshmallows in that bag."

He pointed to another grocery bag, "How about this one?"

"Yup," replied Brianna. "I looked in there."

"Well," he snorted. "Did you look under the table?"

Virginia replied, "Yes Dad, I looked under the table."

Her dad crouched down. As he crawled under the table, Virginia noticed something white stuck to the rear end of his pants. In the darkness it looked like a pillow. Virginia shined her flashlight at the white mass. It looked fluffy. She poked the white blob with her finger. It was soft. She hollered, "I think I found the marshmallows."

"Where?" grunted Virginia's dad from under the table.

The other girls whipped around to see the torn bag of marshmallows stuck to Mr. Hamhock's rear end.

"Eeewww!" shrieked Lacy.

"Gross!" yelled Olivia.

"They're stuck to your pants!" said Virginia.

"What?" asked Mr. Hamhock. He backed out from under the table and pulled the gooey marshmallow mess from the backside of his pants.

He held up the bag of marshmallows. The plastic was ripped to shreds. The large mass of marshmallows was covered with dirt, bark and rocks. Sadly, there would be no s'mores.

Pouting, the girls returned to their log seats next to the campfire.

Mr. Hamhock chucked another log on the fire and sat down. For several minutes there was silence around the campfire.

Virginia's dad tried to interest the girls in another

activity. He suggested, "How about a game of hot potato?"

"Nah," they responded.

"The alphabet game?"

"Uh uh," they moped.

"Another game of telephone?"

"Nope," they sulked.

"How about a ghost story?"

The girls looked up. Everyone loves ghost stories. They couldn't resist.

"Okay, but let's tell it as a circle story," said Franny.

"What's a circle story?" asked Mr. Hamhock.

Virginia explained, "A circle story is when one person starts the story, and everyone else adds to the story when it's their turn."

"Sounds like fun," said Mr. Hamhock.

"Can I start?" asked Franny.

Virginia's dad nodded, "Sure, what's your story?"

Franny thought for a moment and launched into her tale, "About ten years ago, after this campsite was just built, a newlywed couple decided to take a camping trip as their honeymoon."

Mr. Hamhock and the other girls listened intently. The fire crackled as Franny continued.

"On their way here, the couple picked up a hitchhiker. He was crazy looking with bulging eyes and a wicked laugh."

Franny nudged Lacey to let her know it was her turn. Lacey thought a moment, and continued the story.

"As the hitchhiker jumped into the car, the bride thought she saw a piece of hair sticking out of his knapsack. When they were driving down the highway, the hitchhiker told the bride and groom that he had just quit his job at the slaughterhouse."

"No way," blurted Brianna nervously.

"Then what happened?" asked Virginia.

Lacey continued, "As they were driving, the hitchhiker reached into his knapsack." She paused for effect. The other girls leaned forward on their logs. "And pulled out a…" Another pause. The girls were silent with anticipation. "…Jacket. Because he was cold."

There was a sigh of relief and the girls giggled as they realized that Lacey had reeled them in.

Franny said, "I have to go to the bathroom." She stood up from her log and started toward the campground bathroom.

Virginia's dad said, "You can't go to the bathroom alone."

"But I really have to go," squirmed Franny.

"Who'll go with her?" he asked.

The girls looked into the darkness past the edge of the firelight. None of them volunteered.

Mr. Hamhock pointed to Lacey. "Why don't you go with Franny since you've told your part of the story."

Lacey hesitated.

Franny pressed her knees together, "C'mon, Lacey. I'm gonna pee my pants!"

Lacey reluctantly followed Franny into the darkness.

Mr. Hamhock looked at Olivia, "What happened next?"

Olivia resumed the story, "By the time the bride and groom arrived at the campground, it was almost dark. They parked next to the ranger station and knocked on the door. But there was no answer. They went inside and found a steaming cup of coffee sitting next to a ranger's hat on the desk."

Brianna asked, "Where was the ranger?"

"Gone," Olivia answered with an eerie tone of voice. "Disappeared into thin air."

She nodded to Virginia, who continued without skipping a beat, "The bride and groom called out, but there was no answer. They were tired from their long drive and decided to make camp and go to sleep."

"They drove into the campground past the glow of several campfires. But there was no one around. The campground was completely empty, even though there were pitched tents and roaring campfires."

Mr. Hamhock asked, "Where did everyone go?"

Virginia nudged Rebecca. She picked up where Virginia left off, "The couple got out of their car, and looked up at the full moon. They heard the wind whistle through the trees, and a wolf howled in the distance."

Virginia's dad shivered with fear at Rebecca's description and interrupted, "I think maybe we should stop. This story is getting scary. I don't want you girls to have bad dreams."

Virginia protested, "C'mon, Dad. Let her finish."

"Yeah, we won't have bad dreams," added Olivia.

Mr. Hamhock relented, "Okay, but not so scary."

He put another log on the fire.

Rebecca continued, "The couple unpacked their camping gear, and started to pitch their tent by the light of the full moon."

Rebecca nodded to Brianna. As Brianna started

96

to speak, there was a rustling sound in the woods beyond the glow of the fire.

Mr. Hamhock shushed Brianna and whispered, "Did you hear that?"

Virginia began to speak, "I think it was…" Her father shushed her, too.

Mr. Hamhock and the girls listened, but the woods were eerily quiet. They scooted closer together on the log.

Brianna resumed her story, "As the couple set up their tent, the wind blew harder and the trees sounded like they were moaning with pain. A large cloud passed in front of the moon, and the campsite went pitch black. The couple heard a growling sound. It started far off and got closer. And closer…"

As Brianna was about to continue, there was a bloodcurdling scream.

Mr. Hamhock jumped up from his log. As he did, the log shifted. The other four girls fell off backwards.

Virginia's dad yelled, "Run for your lives." He bolted into the darkness.

Franny and Lacey stepped into the light of the fire from the darkness of the woods and yelled, "Gotcha!" They were the ones who had screamed. The other girls burst into laughter.

Campfire Skits

After Mr. Hamhock realized it was Franny and Lacey who screamed, he returned to the campfire. Franny and Lacey meant to scare the other girls, not Virginia's dad. They hoped he wasn't mad.

Mr. Hamhock approached Franny and Lacey. He stood in front of them, casting a flickering shadow across their faces from the campfire. They looked up nervously, expecting him to dole out a punishment for their behavior.

"Franny and Lacey," he said in a stern voice. "That was the best prank anyone has ever pulled on me."

He stuck his hoof out. Franny and Lacey each

slapped him five. They were glad that Virginia's dad had a good sense of humor.

"You should have seen your face," commented Lacey. "

"You looked like you saw a ghost," added Franny.

Virginia chimed in, "It was hilarious, Dad."

"Do me a favor, please don't tell mom," said Mr. Hamhock with a chuckle. "I don't want her to think I'm a wimp."

"Don't worry," said Olivia. "What happens at the campout stays at the campout."

"That was a good ghost story," he admitted. "I'm impressed."

He tossed another log onto the glowing embers in the fire pit and sat back down on his log. "Why don't you tell another story? But this time, make it about what you've learned as scouts today."

"I have an idea," said Olivia.

"Okay, let's hear it," he said.

"When I was at summer camp last year, we performed skits at the final campfire. Maybe we could do some skits about what we learned today."

"That's a great idea," agreed Mr. Hamhock. Why don't you separate into three pairs? Each pair can perform a skit. Virginia and Rebecca, why don't you start. Franny and Lacey, you'll go second. Brianna and Olivia, you'll go third."

The girls buzzed with excitement. This was going to be fun.

"Take a few minutes to think up your skits. I'm going to clean up the dinner table so wild animals won't be tempted to attack our campsite. Let me know when you're ready."

Mr. Hamhock disappeared into the darkness. The girls huddled together to discuss their skits.

Within ten minutes the girls had all planned their skits. They gathered a few props from their duffel bags and told Mr. Hamhock they were ready. Brianna, Olivia, Franny and Lacey took their seats as Virginia and Rebecca prepared to perform first.

Virginia's dad threw several logs on the fire. The flames danced higher, illuminating the area next to the fire pit where the girls would perform.

There was a moment of silence as Mr. Hamhock and the other girls sat on their logs in anticipation. Rebecca appeared from out of the darkness. She pretended to open a box and spoke, "Hey, Dad. Here's the box of camping gear you've been looking for."

Virginia appeared out of the darkness. There was a pillow stuffed under her shirt, giving her a chubby belly. "Don't be a piggy, Virginia. Let me have a look."

The other girls giggled, realizing that Virginia was portraying her father. They snuck a look at Mr. Hamhock. He was grinning from ear to ear, enjoying the performance.

Virginia continued, "Is my sleeping bag in that box?"

"It sure is," replied Rebecca as she pretended to pull the sleeping bag out of the box

Virginia made an exaggerated expression of surprise, "Oh, no. My sleeping bag has been eaten by a bunch of moths. Those moths were piggies."

"They sure were," echoed Mr. Hamhock, enjoying the skit.

"Looks like you'll need a new sleeping bag," replied Rebecca.

"I'll need more than just a sleeping bag," answered Virginia as her father. "Let's go to the Army Supply Store and stock up on camping gear."

"Don't forget the trash bags," added Rebecca.

"Of course not. I wouldn't want to be a piggy," answered Virginia, still pretending to be Mr. Hamhock.

The girls looked over to see Mr. Hamhock's reaction. He shrugged, as if to say, "Hey, I forgot."

Virginia stepped back into the darkness. Rebecca put her hand to her forehead and scanned the horizon, as if looking for something. "Where is Mr. Hamhock? We've been waiting for nearly half an hour." She turned as if speaking to someone else, "Do you think that's piggy behavior?"

Virginia ran into the light of the campfire, acting as though she were out of breath. She carried two duffel bags. "I couldn't fit this stuff on my trailer because I bought everything in the Army Supply Store."

Mr. Hamhock and the other girls hooted with laughter.

Virginia continued, "It's going to be a great campout. I bought a shark cage and a grand piano. C'mon, girls. Let's head to the campground."

Virginia and Rebecca pretended to be driving in the van. They bobbed up and down. They leaned comically to the left as if going around a turn. They leaned to the right as if going around another turn.

Virginia pointed ahead, "There's the campsite."

Rebecca made a disgusted face. "There's garbage all over our campsite."

Virginia pretended to stop the van. She and Rebecca got out.

103

Virginia shook her head, "Looks like someone will have to clean up this mess. Why don't you get started while I take a nap?"

"Wait a second," Rebecca replied. "Isn't that piggy behavior?"

"Only if some one catches me," admitted Virginia as her father.

The rest of the scouts burst into laughter.

Mr. Hamhock protested comically, "I didn't mean to fall asleep. I was tired from driving."

Rebecca and Virginia bowed. The other scouts applauded. Next, it was Franny and Lacey's turn. They got up from their seats and disappeared into the darkness beyond the campfire.

As the scouts waited, Virginia looked over at her father. "Sorry, Dad. It's all in fun."

Mr. Hamhock smiled, "I guess I deserve a little ribbing. I was late, and I should have helped you girls clean up the campsite."

From the darkness, Lacey called out, "Act two."

"Virginia, this campsite is a mess. I'm going to talk to the Ranger," said Franny as she walked into the light of the campfire, wearing a pillow under her shirt. Now she was portraying Mr. Hamhock.

Franny pretended to get into an invisible minivan. She began stepping backwards as though driving the minivan in reverse. Lacey stepped into the light of the campfire and yelled, "Watch out, you're going to run over our neighbor's campsite."

Franny continued backing up. Rebecca yelled from the crowd, "Watch out."

Olivia joined in, "You're heading straight for that campsite."

Lacey pretended to watch Franny crash the trailer into the neighbor's campsite.

"Looks like someone might mistake that piggy for a bear," said Lacey, pointing to Franny as Mr. Hamhock.

As Virginia's dad watched the skit, it dawned on him what had really happened. He looked at the girls and asked, "There was never a bear attack, was there?"

The girls shook their heads no.

He continued, "I ran over our neighbor's campsite with my trailer, didn't I?"

The girls nodded.

Mr. Hamhock sighed, "I can't believe I did that. And I didn't even realize."

Franny broke the solemn mood, commenting, "Driving a vehicle with trailer is tricky. You can't expect to master it in just one day."

Virginia's dad smiled. He appreciated that the

girls realized he'd made a mistake.

Franny got out of the invisible minivan and walked past Lacey, "I'm going to take another nap. Wake me when you're finished pitching the tent."

The scouts laughed loudly. Mr. Hamhock laughed the loudest.

Lacey pretended to pitch the tent, but gave up, calling out, "Mr. Hamhock, can you help me pitch this tent?"

From the darkness came a reply, "I'm trying to sleep. Plus, I would probably just rip a hole in the side."

The girls roared with laughter.

Virginia's dad cried out in mock protest, "C'mon, I only fell asleep once."

Franny joined Lacey in front of the fire. They bowed and the audience applauded.

Finally, it was time for Brianna and Olivia. They hopped off their logs, trading places with Franny and Lacey next to the campfire. Brianna stepped backward until she was out of sight in the darkness. Olivia held her wings up as though looking through a pair of binoculars.

"Look, there's a Pterodactyl," pointed Olivia. "The first one that's been spotted in two million years. Let me get my camera so I can take a picture."

Olivia pretended to grab her camera. "Hold still Mr. Pterodactyl. I just want one photo."

Suddenly, from out of the darkness, Brianna yelled, "C'mon girls. We have to get back to camp. The football game starts in two minutes."

Mr. Hamhock and the girls laughed wildly.

Brianna stepped into the light of the campfire. There was a pillow stuffed under her shirt. Now, she was pretending to be Mr. Hamhock. Frustrated, Olivia raised her wings in the air, "You scared the Pterodactyl away. I could have sold that picture for a million dollars."

Brianna apologized, "I didn't realize you were trying to take a picture. I'll make it up to you. Why don't you join us for dinner?"

"What are you having?" asked Olivia.

Brianna answered, "Log Pop soup and dandelion salad."

"Yum! I love Log Pop soup!"

The scouts howled with laughter, and clapped for Olivia and Brianna's performance. Mr. Hamhock clapped the loudest.

After the applause finished, Olivia and Brianna returned to their seats on the log. Virginia's dad stood up and spoke, "I'd like to apologize for all my piggy behavior today. I never imagined that my actions would affect others so negatively."

"It's okay, Dad," said Virginia.

"No it's not," replied her dad. "I was supposed to set a good example on this camping trip. Instead, I broke scout rules, destroyed our neighbor's campsite, ripped a hole in your tent, and ruined our dinner. I hope you girls can forgive me."

"Of course we forgive you," said Olivia.

"We know you didn't mean to be a piggy," added Brianna.

"We didn't really want s'mores anyway," said Lacey.

"Umm, yes we did," protested Rebecca.

"I wish I hadn't sat on the marshmallows," answered Virginia's dad. "I love s'mores."

He stepped toward his log, but stopped and smiled, "I have an idea. It's pretty crazy but it just might work. Find me a long stick about an inch in diameter. I'll be back in a second."

The girls sprang into action. They searched the dwindling woodpile and found the perfect stick. Mr. Hamhock returned with the bag of squashed marshmallows. He pulled the shredded plastic off. The mass of marshmallows was covered with dirt, sticks and rocks.

"You know what this is?" he asked.

Virginia replied, "A disgusting mess."

"You're right. But it's also the world's biggest marshmallow. Did you find a stick?"

Franny handed Mr. Hamhock the stick. He poked the huge marshmallow with the stick and held it up for the girls to see, "We're going to roast the world's largest marshmallow."

He held the huge marshmallow over the fire until the outside turned a crispy golden brown. Then he pulled it out of the fire and asked Virginia to hold the stick.

"How do you think we're going to get this marshmallow clean?" asked Mr. Hamhock.

"Peel off the outer layer!" yelled Franny.

"That's right," replied Virginia's dad. He grabbed the huge marshmallow with his hands and peeled the outside layer off. With it came the dirt, sticks and rocks. That left fresh marshmallow. The girls couldn't believe it. Virginia's dad was a genius!

Virginia handed the stick back to her dad. He smiled and said, "Who wants s'mores?"

The girls cheered, "We do!"

As Mr. Hamhock roasted the huge marshmallow over the fire, the girls tore open the graham crackers and chocolate bars.

When the giant marshmallow was golden brown,

Virginia's dad swung it away from the fire. The girls each grabbed a piece of the marshmallow with their graham crackers and sandwiched it with the chocolate.

Within a few minutes, the marshmallow had melted the chocolate. The girls enjoyed the best s'mores they'd ever eaten.

Scout Badges

As Virginia ate her s'more, she looked across the fire. The flames illuminated her dad's face.

He smiled and raised his water bottle. "Here's to being resourceful. I'm really proud of you girls. You did a great job salvaging dinner."

The girls raised their water bottles in a toast. He continued, "And you did a great job cleaning up the campsite. The piggies that camped here last night really left a mess. We have to do everything we can to stop piggy behavior. I think that you've learned that on this camping trip." He chuckled, "You certainly busted me for my piggy behavior."

"All in all, I'd say this was a very successful

camping trip." He leaned back against his log. The scouts kicked back and enjoyed the crackling fire.

Olivia looked up at the sky and exclaimed, "Look, a shooting star!"

The others looked up to see a star shoot across the sky, leaving a long glowing tail.

Franny pointed, "There's the Big Dipper."

"And the Little Dipper," said Lacey.

Mr. Hamhock pointed to another constellation, "There's Orion. You can see the three stars that form his belt. Orion is a hunter in Greek mythology."

"Next to Orion is Taurus the bull," pointed Brianna. "That large star is his head. Those two smaller stars are the tips of his horns."

"What's that foggy area?" asked Virginia, pointing upwards.

Her dad replied, "That's the Milky Way, a galaxy that contains hundreds of billions of stars."

"Wow, I've never seen that before."

"That's because it's normally drowned out by the lights of the city," he replied. "The Milky Way is so faint, you can only see it when you're away from the city lights."

Mr. Hamhock and the girls spent the next half hour pointing out constellations and talking about Greek mythology.

113

By the time the scouts finished their discussion the fire had died down. The flames were gone and the coals glowed orange in the fire pit.

"You girls really know a lot about constellations," said Virginia's dad. "I think you might qualify for your Sky Search badge."

Badges. The girls had been so busy, they had forgotten about their badges.

Virginia didn't want to think about badges. The campout was her last chance to earn the eight badges she needed to graduate to Cadette Scout.

She had kidded herself to think that she could earn eight badges in one day. Margaret Oxley earned eight and she was as close to perfect as any girl Virginia had ever met.

Virginia was saddened by the thought that all her friends would be Cadette Scouts in the sixth grade while she would be left behind. There would be no more troop meetings or camping trips for her.

Mr. Hamhock pulled out his clipboard and turned his flashlight on to read, "According to this list, there are several badges that you girls were working on during this camping trip."

The scouts listened intently as he continued, "First, the Camping badge."

The girls weren't sure if they had satisfied the

requirements for the Camping badge. Brianna crossed her claws. Olivia crossed her wings.

"You girls made a valiant effort. You tried to pitch your tent, but I messed that up when I ripped it with the tent pole. You did a great job building the fire. I'm sure the spaghetti and garlic bread would have turned out delicious if I hadn't put too many logs on."

"I'm submitting all of your names for the Camping badge."

The scouts cheered.

Mr. Hamhock looked at the badge list on his clipboard and continued, "Next, is the Arts and Crafts badge."

The girls smiled. They felt confident that their arts and crafts project would earn them a badge.

"You did a fantastic job on your nature frames and I was impressed by the originality of each of your drawings. Congratulations on satisfying the requirements for the Arts and Crafts badge."

The girls gave each other a round of high fives.

Mr. Hamhock continued, "According to Mrs. Oxley's records, Franny needed two badges in order to graduate to Cadette Scout. Congratulations Franny, you made it."

Franny grinned from pointed ear to pointed

ear. Olivia and Lacey clapped her on the back. Mr. Hamhock looked down at his clipboard.

"Next, is the Hiker badge. There's no doubt in my mind that you all earned it. Those switchbacks and log bridge were a real challenge. Congratulations, Brianna. You'll be a Cadette Scout next year since you earned three badges."

Mr. Hamhock gave Brianna a thumbs up.

"Next, the Plants and Animals badge. I was scared at the thought we might see a real bear after the Ranger told us about the attack on our neighbor's campsite. Fortunately, it was only some piggy trying to back up a trailer."

The scouts laughed.

"You successfully identified a number of trees in the forest, wildflowers in the meadow and edible plants for our dinner. In addition, you saw several wild animals, including one of the rarest birds in North America. I hereby award you the Plants and Animals badge. Rebecca, you'll graduate to Cadette Scout next year."

Rebecca grinned. The other scouts congratulated her. She looked at Virginia, who gave her a half-hearted smile. Virginia was happy for her friend, but sad knowing that she would fall short of the thirty badges needed for Cadette Scout.

Her father continued, "After I botched our dinner this evening, I figured that you girls could kiss the Outdoor Cook badge goodbye, but you rallied with resourcefulness and resolve. I'm going to recommend Log Pop soup for future campouts."

The scouts laughed at Mr. Hamhock's reference to their makeshift dinner.

"And the dandelion trail mix salad was nutritional and healthy. Congratulations on earning your Outdoor Cook badge! It looks like Olivia and Lacey will graduate to Cadette Scout next year."

That left Virginia. She looked at the other girls. They were smiling, happy with themselves for earning the thirty badges. Virginia was still short three badges.

Her dad spoke again, "I have the complete list of badges here and I'm proud to say that you've all satisfied the requirements for the Sky Search badge. That's a total of six badges you earned on this campout. I'm very proud of you."

It didn't matter that Virginia had earned six badges on the campout. She was still two badges shy of making Cadette Scout. Virginia couldn't contain herself any longer. She burst into tears and darted into the darkness.

No one knew what to do, except Rebecca. She

rushed after her friend.

Rebecca found Virginia sitting next to the minivan. Her head was buried in her arms and she sobbed quietly. Rebecca knelt down next to Virginia and said, "You can have two of my badges. I've got a couple of extra ones."

Virginia looked up and smiled at her best friend. Rebecca continued, "If you hadn't gotten sick with the flu, you'd have enough badges to make Cadette Scout. Maybe Mrs. Oxley will give you another chance."

Virginia shook her head, "Mrs. Oxley is strict. I don't think she'd give her own daughter another chance. Not that Margaret would need it. I guess I'll just concentrate on sports and music next year since I won't make Cadette Scout."

"Well, if you're not going to be in scouts, I'm not going to be in scouts. It wouldn't be any fun without you."

Rebecca stood and extended her paw to help Virginia up. Suddenly, they heard yelling from the campfire.

"Virginia, come here," yelled her dad.

"Yeah, come quick," echoed the other girls.

Virginia jumped up. She and Rebecca rushed toward the campfire as the other scouts called, "You

118

have to check this out."

Rebecca and Virginia arrived to find a roaring campfire. The other scouts had used the rest of the wood.

Virginia's dad pointed at his clipboard and announced, "The girls and I doubled checked the master badge list and found something interesting." He looked at the other scouts and they smiled in support. "Given that you all created those wonderful campfire skits, you're eligible for the Theatre badge."

Virginia looked at her dad and squealed, "Really?"

"Yes, honey."

Virginia's smile faded, "I still need one badge."

Her dad continued, "Well, there's a badge called Eco-Action. By cleaning up our trashed campsite, your troop satisfied the requirements. I'm going to submit your names for the Eco-Action badge. That raises the number of badges you earned on this campout to a total of eight."

The scouts could hardly believe what he was saying. Eight badges! That was the same number that Margaret Oxley earned when she set the record. The girls had tied Margaret Oxley for the most badges earned on a campout.

Mr. Hamhock smiled, "Now you have a total of thirty badges. You'll graduate to Cadette Scout with the rest of the troop. Congratulations."

Virginia couldn't believe it. Those eight badges gave her the thirty badges she needed to graduate to Cadette Scout the following year. She had done it!

The scouts hollered and whooped with excitement. Rebecca hugged Virginia, excited that they would both be Cadette Scouts in sixth grade.

Mr. Hamhock shushed the scouts and said, "Let's keep it down, we don't want to be piggies and wake our neighboring campers."

The girls reduced their volume. Virginia's dad looked down at the clipboard. A grin spread across his face.

"You're not going to believe this," he said to the scouts. "There's a badge called Creative Solutions."

The girls looked at him blankly. He continued, "After I ruined the dinner, you came up with an alternate menu using lunch leftovers and wild dandelions. That was a creative solution to our dinner dilemma."

The scouts nodded as Virginia's dad continued, "Based on your creation of Log Pop soup and dandelion salad, I'm nominating all of you for the Creative Solutions badge. That raises the number of badges that you earned on this campout to a whopping total of nine badges! Congratulations girls, you now hold the record for the most badges ever earned on a campout."

The girls could hardly believe it. Nine badges. That was one more than Margaret Oxley's record!

The girls danced around the campfire in a conga line, kicking up their legs and waving their arms from side to side. The second time around, Mr. Hamhock joined their celebratory dance. The flames of the fire cast a yellow glow on the smiling faces of the scouts and their leader, Mr. Hamhock.

They danced several times more around the campfire then stopped, exhausted. Virginia's dad looked up at the stars and commented, "Clear skies tonight. No chance of rain. Let's grab our sleeping bags and sleep by the fire."

The scouts nodded in agreement, and headed to the minivan to get their sleeping bags.

Within minutes, Mr. Hamhock and the scouts were nestled in their sleeping bags near the glowing fire with a sky full of stars shining down on them.

Virginia looked over at her father and said, "Thanks, Dad. This was the best campout ever!"

PIGGY NATION
DISCUSSION QUESTIONS

1. What is piggy behavior?
2. What did Mr. Hamhock do that was piggy behavior?
3. What could Mr. Hamhock have done after he was a piggy?
   Apologize or offer to correct the problem
4. What was thoughtful about the way Virginia and the other scouts told Mr. Hamhock about his piggy behavior?
5. What piggy behavior has someone done to you?
6. How did you feel afterward?
7. What should you do when someone is a piggy?
   Ignore the piggy
   Ask the person to stop their piggy behavior
   Write the person a Piggy Ticket
8. Have you ever been a piggy?
9. What did you do that was piggy behavior?
10. What could you have done instead?
11. What will you do next time you're a piggy?
    Apologize or offer to correct the problem
12. What other piggy behavior can you think of?
13. What can you do to prevent piggy behavior?
14. Make your own Piggy Ticket

PIGGY NATION ACTIVITIES WORD SEARCH

```
N C R T R U D E S D F A E
A O B N O X I O U S J P L
F N P H E L P F U L K O I
G S T H O U G H T F U L R
P I G G Y B E H A V I O R
O D W S T P D F G H J G I
L E U Y I R A G M L K I T
I R N I C E N T X C V Z A
T A F H K I N D R T R E T
E T F H E J O P E O P D E
M E S S T K Y L I T L E R
```

MESS	RUDE	NICE
POLITE	KIND	ANNOY
APOLOGIZE	HELPFUL	IRRITATE
THOUGHTFUL	CONSIDERATE	OBNOXIOUS
PIGGYBEHAVIOR	PIGGYTICKET	PIGGYPATROL

CAMPING STORY

You and a friend can take Virginia's scout troop
on a crazy camping adventure!
Fill in the blanks and read the hilarious new story.

Mr. Hamhock drove Virginia's scout troop to the

_____ in his _____. When they arrived,
(place)   (type of transportation)

_____ were scattered everywhere. The scouts
(things)

started cleaning with a _____. They saw a wild
(noun)

_____ and called the _____. For
(animal)   (type of job)

dinner, the scouts cooked _____ and _____.
(food)   (food)

Afterwards, they roasted _____ over the _____.
(type of candy)   (thing)

124